Divided
and
Other Stories

H. Rad Bethlen

Rooster & Raven

For the Daughters of Zeus and Mnemosyne

Author Statement Concerning Artificial Intelligence

The way I write consist of several phases.

1. Idea generation.
2. Research.
3. Story development.
4. Outlining.
5. Writing the rough draft.
6. Editing and rewriting.
7. Editing and polishing.
8. Copy editing.

I will *occasionally* use AI during the research phase if I can't locate some bit of information on my own—but I try to locate it on my own first.

I will *occasionally* use AI during the story's development if I get stuck on something—but I try to resolve my own story issues first.

I *intentionally* use AI during the copy editing phase as a stand-in for a copy editor, which I can't afford to pay for yet which I don't want to go without.

A copy editor is the last set of eyes to look at a manuscript to check for grammar, usage, spelling, and punctuation mistakes. I ask the AI copy editor to make suggestions on corrections. I evaluate those suggestions. If I agree, I make the changes.

I don't use AI for anything else.

Be comforted that these stories were written by a human being for other human beings.

H. Rad Bethlen

Divided

Professor Amy Hale stood in the archway, looking. There was nothing to see. The white walls were free of even nail holes. She leaned back and turned her head. The gallery next to hers had been hung. She wasn't sure who the artist was. She avoided looking at the label. She was afraid she might know them. The walls were covered with enormous replicas of crumpled candy wrappers; Snickers, Charleston Chew, Mounds, Milk Duds, etc. She had no idea what to make of it.

'Is this art?' she asked herself. 'Or some kind of commentary on the gluttony and wastefulness of consumer culture?' She looked to her latte and frowned. She looked back to the wrappers. 'No, it's a critique of the obesity epidemic, gotta be.' She thought of Rembrandt shivering in his studio, painting the wrinkles of his own face as he saw them in the mirror. She thought of Georgia O'Keeffe on a mountain precipice, the sun cooking her skin, her eyes ablaze with the colors of the desert. 'Ah, a commentary about the influence of pop art on modern design.' She prided herself on the fact that her art didn't need instructions, although she had been losing pride in even that.

She had a hard time pulling her eyes from the brilliant blue of the Baby Ruth. 'It's too easy,' she thought. 'It's intellectual gobbledygook in place of craft, feeling, personal insight, vision, beauty. It's completely un-compelling. Looking at it makes me feel absolutely nothing.' She looked for and found the artist's statement. 'I'm sure all of the emotional content is spelled out there,' she thought. She looked back to the vibrant blue of the Baby Ruth. 'It's well made,' she observed. 'There's an attention to detail, clear lines, a certain playfulness, and the crumpling provides an element of texture and three dimensionality. It has that going for it.' She let her eyes scan the gallery.

She began to wonder what would become of a six-foot wide, two-foot tall Charleston Chew wrapper once the exhibit was over. Would someone buy it? She left the embrace of the archway, walked over to the painting, and looked at the business-card-sized rectangle of paper pinned to the wall beneath it.

"Chewed," it said.

'Clever,' she thought.

"$2500," the card read.

She glanced at it. She doubted that a private collector would ever buy such a thing. Perhaps when pop art had first appeared, when Andy Warhol printed *32 Campbell's Soup Cans*, it was novel enough to attract serious collectors. That was in 1962. Even though Warhol was dead going on thirty years, he still had his imitators.

'Some institution will buy it,' she thought. 'Two grand is cheap when you're spending tax payer money.' She studied it.

"You'll collect dust in all of your crevices," she said to the painting. "I wonder if the janitor will wipe you clean from time to time?" Of course not, janitors never touched the art. She thought of the artist.

She wondered if he or she would ever desire to see the piece again after it was sold. She wondered if a maker of giant candy bar wrappers ever missed those "paintings" that disappeared into hallways and homes. She still missed her early paintings. They were like children grown older— gone into the world to make it on their own.

She cherished the memories that those paintings anchored. They were, like the bare, grass-whipped columns of Athens, markers of past glory. She thought of the most recent painting she sold. It went to a community college down state. She struggled to remember the specifics of the canvas. She struggled to remember painting it. In the absence of recall her mind substituted: emails from students, departmental meetings, uninspired lesson plans. Underneath those things was a stark truth, she hated it all. Her mind tried to hide it but she knew, had known for years.

'All chewed up,' she thought. She returned to her gallery space. It was thirteen feet wide, ten feet deep, seven foot ten inches from floor to ceiling, three walls and an archway.

Weeks ago, she had received an email that stated the space was 1018.33 cubic feet. She could do as she liked, with special accommodations available for installation art; liquids or gasses would be considered, provided they be inert.

'I just want to hang paintings,' she thought. She questioned her own creativity. She had never conceived a piece of art that involved gases or liquids, inert or otherwise, except for paint. 'Maybe something's wrong with me,' she wondered, when she first read the email.

Her paintings were stacked up on the floor in the center of the room, a baker's dozen in all. Nothing separated the paintings, protected their surfaces, no paper or cloth to prevent damage. Acrylic was durable enough that she didn't bother. That's what she told herself but the truth was she didn't care.

She didn't care about her art all that much anymore. They weren't her children; to be developed and nurtured, to be shielded from the cruelty of the outside world, to be protected until they could fend for themselves, then released like wild birds returning to nature, beating wings, lifting up into flight and freedom, into O'Keeffe's brilliant sun.

Now they were work. Now they paid the bills.

She had a new car, a hatchback, so she didn't have to stuff her paintings into the trunk with the spare tire. Thinking about her new purchase transported her back to the days when she was a starving artist.

She hadn't yet gone to university, much to her parents' chagrin. She lived in a studio apartment. It had once been the living room of a large home—now divided. She even had a non-working fireplace. It was a shame it didn't work because she couldn't afford heat in the winter. She wore her father's old Carhartt overalls when she painted. She had even hung a print of Rembrandt's self portrait from 1659 above the mantle. She could still make out the infinite depth in his eyes when she closed hers.

"Here we are again, old man, just the two of us," she used to say.

She could have asked her parents to help and they would have. The money may or may not come with a lecture about the economic repercussions of being an artist. She thought of it as paying her dues. She thought of Vincent, the artist's artist, filling notebooks with crude drawings, so burning up with the fire of creation he didn't feel the cold. He never complained of cold in his letters to Theo, his brother and sponsor. She allowed her own poverty to lend a certain romance to her past. The memories made her smile.

Not that she wanted to go back to those days. To do so was folly. She was a grown up now, not some kid. She had responsibilities. It was adult living, adult compromise. She understood her parents now, understood their concerns and their warnings. When she was a young starving artist she thought her parents had fallen into a trap. They had compromised themselves into a prison. Back then she was dead set against it.

'Maybe I'm just grumpy,' she lamented.

Next to her stack of paintings was a three-legged table on which sat her car keys, purse, and coffee. She took a sip of her latte. She sat down in the chair. 'You should have married rich.' She scolded herself. That thought had been invading her head for a while. 'Hemingway married rich—twice. Clever fellow.' It went against everything she believed as a feminist.

"This is my kept woman, Amy."

"Oh, nice to meet you. Wait, didn't you do that painting in the board room?"

"Yes I did!"

She smiled. It was too late for the fairytale ending. Not that she actually wanted something like that. She had a "domestic partner." Samantha was as supportive as a non-artist could be to an artist. No worries there. Amy suddenly realized she and Samantha hadn't discussed art, hers or any one else's, in quite some time. There had been plenty of complaining about the administration, the students, grants and funding, publishing and showing—the grind.

'I didn't even show you lucky number thirteen,' she realized, her eyes glancing at the painting on top of the stack. She felt bad for Samantha. She recalled taking Samantha to the most recent student exhibition. The night was fine, it was what it was, but it had been a tough night for her personally. She knew that the students weren't getting the best of her. She couldn't see much of interest or promise in the student work. It had to be there. 'Am I too jaded to see it?' she asked herself. Samantha had tried to cheer her up. She held her hand, complimented her dress, kissed her in the corner, near a particularly strange *thing* made out of forest detritus.

She made Samantha stop at a convenience store on the way home. She went in alone, in her skimpy black dress, bought a pack of Camels, pulled one and smoked it at the back corner of the car, facing away. She didn't want Samantha looking at her just then, or really, she didn't want to see Samantha looking at her. She kept the pack in her glittery little purse. It was still there. The rest of the cigarettes unsmoked. She remembered that the "party purse," as Samantha had called it, was still in the car. She decided she needed another cigarette.

"No, hang your paintings," she said out loud.

With a heavy sigh she rose from the chair and walked over to the stack. She looked down at them. She looked away. She reached for her keys and coffee, picked them up, turned and walked outside. She found the new hatchback, found the purse, and found the Camels. She stood, leaned against the car, and smoked. She took long, deep drags. As the smoke curled from her mouth to her nose she imagined the smell of Georgia O'Keeffe's sun-burnt skin. She imagined making love to her, their bodies splattered with paint and lust. She looked past the brick facades of the buildings surrounding the quad, past the color-turned leaves of the trees, past the power lines, to the autumn sun.

'Almost Thanksgiving break,' she thought. Samantha was going home and she, the time-crunched art professor, was staying home, to start a new painting. A sudden urgency struck her. She looked at her wristwatch.

"Oh, shit!" She flicked the Camel and ran back towards the gallery building.

She yanked open the first glass door, stopped before the second. They were crowded in the archway. She closed her eyes and let out a sigh. 'Well, shit,' she thought and opened her eyes. She pulled open the second glass door, preparing the speech in her head. 'Don't panic. Make up some excuse.'

Suddenly, a desire to turn and walk out overcame her. The emotion was so strong she lost her balance. They hadn't noticed her. They stood in the archway, silent, curious. She could imagine their thoughts. Had there been some emergency? No, she left her purse. Did she really not hang her show? Where is she?

"Amy."

One of them said to the rest. Had it been a statement, a question, a condemnation?

Amy stood a dozen feet behind them, paralyzed by the epiphany she was having. Looking at the backs of her fellow "artists," to their right a room full of giant crumpled candy wrappers, caused the illusion to fall away.

'You've lost it. You've lost your honesty, your voice, your creativity.' Her heart sank. 'You've been treading water for years.' The truth of it was tired of being denied. It stood there with her peers, who had come to review the show, before the crowd at the opening made art viewing impossible. Amy was overcome by regret, regret for going to university, regret for having stayed in that ecosystem ever since.

'Who's trapped now?'

She got angry. She stomped forward, parted the group, intending to grab her purse, but she was so emotional, her movements so wild, she knocked it over. 'Fuck!' She screamed in her mind. She felt uncontrolled. She spun, ready to abandon her purse, to flee the gallery altogether, but the rubber soles of her shoes stopped her mid-turn. She was facing her stack of paintings. She was overcome. She kicked her paintings over, scattering them.

"Fuck you," she yelled at the thirteen uninspired paintings, at herself, really. She heard gasps from the onlookers. She turned her head. "Fuck you, too!" she screamed. The sound echoed around the room then slipped out under the archway to hide behind the Milk Duds. She felt tears in her eyes and perspiration on her forehead. She was stunned by her own actions. She blinked away the tears. It was all too much to think about. She squared her shoulders and walked proudly forward.

'If you are going to fuck up your entire career, flush a decade of hard work and compromise down the toilet, at least don't look pathetic,' she told herself. She walked past them without a word. When she got to the door she paused. 'What have you done?' a frightened voice within her asked. She trembled when she thought of the repercussions. She turned and started back. She was prepared to drop to her knees and beg for forgiveness.

"...a meta commentary about traditional art giving way to performance art?"

They had begun to critique her.

"I think it denotes the artist's struggle at that moment when their art becomes a commodity. She *did* knock over her purse."

Sounds of agreement.

"Or the challenge one has when they confront the state of their individual oeuvre at its midway point."

"Isn't she up for tenure?"

"Yes, do you think she is making a commentary on that process?"

"We should consider it."

"This is more complicated than it originally appeared."

Amy started laughing.

The group turned and regarded her.

"A brave departure from your previous work." Commented one, a woman she had seen at conferences, but whose name she had never learned.

"I assume you plan to reproduce the performance tonight at the opening?" asked another, a professor at a private university nearby.

Amy did not answer. She politely made her way past them into the gallery, knelt, gathered the contents of her purse, rose and turned to face them.

"Ladies and gentlemen," she said. "My next performance will involve both liquids and gases, inert, of course."

The group looked impressed. They parted for her and she walked past them, smiling. She went out to her new car. As she glanced up at the oranges, reds, and golds of the leaves she thought of Thanksgiving break and the painting she had in mind.

The Price

Samuel watched the black hair slither through the abandoned salad: a snake, emerging from a sea of honey mustard Dijon dressing, climbing onto a jetty of red cabbage. The knocking of glasses and the tinny sound of silverware clanking interrupted his vigil over the bewildered serpent. He shifted his gaze.

A purse—one side showing Alice and the Queen of Hearts discussing white roses painted red and face-down playing cards, the other side showing vertical black and white stripes—plowed aside the trappings of a meal.

Samuel shifted his gaze yet again, from a perplexed Alice to the jumbled contents of the open purse. The check was splayed out on top of the mass of receipts, crumpled cigarette packs, makeup accessories, and many things he could not identify. The rectangle on the right side boxed-in the amount: $13,612.01. The pay to the order line read: Carrie Kim.

He looked up from the check to the woman sitting across from him. She was taller than him and broader. She retained something of the Amazon's assertive presence and vigorous beauty, despite the ruin of alcohol. She ran a hand through her hair. As she tossed the black mass behind her, several snakes broke free and floated away—mini Quetzalcoatls taking flight, each seeking a private Cortez to welcome ashore.

"How did Poe die again?"

"What?" asked Samuel. Her question had come from so out of the blue it had not registered.

"Price loves Poe," she added.

Samuel sat back in the upholstered chair. "Alcohol poisoning, I think. Something like that."

"I remember," she said. "It was called 'cooping.' Some form of voter fraud. Price said they found Poe dressed in someone else's clothing as he was dying in the gutter. A brilliant writer like that, man-handled, forced," she shook her head, "a shame." She reached into the Alice purse and dug out a cigarette. "Do you like my nails?" she asked. "French manicure, Price's favorite."

"Um," Samuel tried to focus, to stick to the point of the meeting. He'd been mentally absent this entire time while she talked on and on. He chided himself, telling himself to be a professional or risk losing a valuable client. "I can't believe we made that mistake. Usually, we can keep a pen name and a real name separate. I will have accounting write another check. I should have caught it; I apologize." He started to rise. He wanted to get back to the office. "You know," he said. "Everything can be set up automatically. You would get a deposit every quarter."

"I like the checks." A cloud of emotion crossed her face, worrying her features. Samuel didn't really want to enquire, but he couldn't avoid it. He was supposed to care, even if he found her company emotionally draining. He sat back down.

"What is it?"

"What were the sales for Price's last book?"

Samuel shook his head. "I don't know. Price Milner isn't my client."

"Can't you find out? You're in the business."

"I could look at BookScan, but those numbers aren't," he searched for the correct way to describe it, "they only count one sales channel. Online sellers don't report their numbers. BookScan only gets the brick-and-mortar retailers."

"Do you think it did well? I heard his sales haven't been as good since *Fame* was published."

'*Fame*,' thought Samuel. 'Price won a National Book Award for that.'

"What ever happened to the movie?" he asked, his curiosity getting the better of him. "You said they were going to make a movie out of it."

"Price didn't like the cast or director."

"Usually writers don't have a say. They sell the rights, and that's that."

She chuckled. "You don't know Price. He would rather be poor and have integrity than be rich and compromise." She looked at Samuel. "I mean, he *is* a Leo."

Samuel couldn't help but smile. 'A Leo,' he thought, 'ridiculous.'

"I don't want to out-sell him."

Samuel looked at her, then to the check, then back to her. "Not many authors see royalty checks like that—or royalty checks at all. Your sales are going through the roof. You're already on the *New York Times* best sellers list."

"Price has been too!" she said, defending him from a perceived attack.

"Ashley," he said, "you're probably going to the top of the list. There's a lot of interest in your book right now. It's a sleeper hit, totally unexpected. The publisher's freaking out, putting pressure on the printers. I don't have the numbers yet, but," he paused. He didn't want to speak too soon, it was his responsibility, though, to prepare her, "your next royalty check could be high five digits, maybe six."

She blushed.

"I hope to get a call from Hollywood. I can't promise that," he said, holding up his hands. "Although, I could see a made-for-TV-movie. Everyone is throwing money around."

She blanched.

"That's a good thing, Ashley. That's what we want."

"Why did you want me to write it under an alias anyway? If you wanted a call from Hollywood? Won't they find out who I am?"

"The entire idea is to 'find you out.' If people feel like they're getting in on a secret they love it that much more. When your true identity becomes known sales will spike."

"It makes it seem like I'm hiding," she shot back.

"We talked about this, remember? It's how the game is played."

"I don't like it," she said, frowning. "Price is going to think I was trying to hide. You know that's not what I wanted." She looked at Samuel. She reached up and put the cigarette between her lips. "I need to smoke."

Samuel picked up the faux leather folder that contained the bill. "I'll email you when the check goes in the mail." He smiled. "This time, I'll take a look at it before the agency mails it off."

The pair rose. This wasn't the type of place that had a cash register at the front door. He could have waited for the server to return to the table, but that would give his client more time to fret and worry and talk about her ex, Price Milner.

Despite his fear, she moved toward the door, leaving the table without a word. There was a bare spot where the Alice purse had been. The absence struck him. He didn't dwell on it but found the server and paid.

He stopped at the coat check and gathered his coat and scarf. It was October in New York City, which meant it was already cold. He gazed out of the window as he donned his coat, watching the people hurrying past. He turned and made his way out, hands in his pockets. An arm slid underneath his as the door shut behind him.

"I still love him."

Samuel turned.

"I love him. I don't want to hurt him."

"I don't see how your memoir hurts him."

Ashley pulled him into motion. "There's some crazy shit in there."

"Life is crazy, especially an artist's life. Price knows that."

Ashley looked at him, then returned her gaze to the sidewalk ahead of them. "I don't think he cares about fame or money," she said. Her tone was respectful but at the same time sorrowful, as if she felt he was right, but right in the way a martyr is right. "When I met him he was flat broke. He was even homeless for awhile."

"I know, I've read your book."

"Oh, yeah, right." She tried to smile but didn't quite get it going. "It was his idea." She tossed the butt of the cigarette into the gutter. "The book—he told me years ago that I should write a book."

"It's good that you wrote it. I know all of this is intimidating but it's for the best."

"Is it?" she asked, looking at him. "I don't know that it is."

"Don't you want to be on *Ellen*?"

"I'd feel like Adele. A fat girl with a pretty face who made it big. I would have to lose weight, like she did, when she put out her second album."

Samuel nodded, although he wasn't up to speed on Adele.

"She gained it all back," Ashley said, reaching into her purse to produce another cigarette. "I hope the smoke doesn't bother you." She placed the cigarette between her lips.

Samuel smiled. 'You can smoke like a chimney,' he thought, 'as long as you earn.'

Ashley disentangled her arm from his. She shielded the tip of the cigarette from the wind and lit it. She dropped the lighter into her purse. Her arm snaked back into place.

"I didn't think anyone would read the thing. I wish I hadn't written it."

Samuel looked at her. "Really?" He assumed she had already considered the fact that people would read her book.

"Price used to read me all of these articles about the percentage of writers who make it. The number of writers who actually earn a living from writing alone." She glanced over at Samuel but looked away. "He wrote three novels before *Fame*. Nobody read any of them, not even me. They sat on his computer, orphans. He spent three years on the first one. I can't even imagine that—spending three years writing a book no one will ever read."

"Its a tough discipline."

Ashley chuckled. "You don't understand." She looked at him. "I don't mean to be a bitch, but you'd never understand a person like Price."

"I know lots of writers," said Samuel. "I am a literary agent."

"Right," said Ashley. She snorted air through her nostrils. "I know everything about him. I remember everything he ever said to me, everything he ever did." She drew in a lungful of smoke and let it out. "It was easy to write that part of the book, Price's part," she said. "I just poured it out like water—word water."

"It's like that some times," observed Samuel.

"Good thing I had help with all of the rest," she laughed, tugging him off balance with her arm. "Thanks for that."

Samuel looked at her, "For introducing you to Justine?"

"Yeah, she's my person." Ashley looked to Samuel. "She gets checks, too, right?"

"She got a flat fee."

"I wish we had put her name on the cover."

"It's your life."

The pair walked for a while in silence. They reached the entrance of the building that housed the agency. He paused. He pulled his right hand from his pocket, bent it at the elbow, and checked his watch. "I have a meeting—"

"I wrote it for him," she interrupted. "I mean, I wrote it to," she looked at Samuel, "to tell him that I still love him. That I think about him every day. That it sucks to live without him. I wanted him to know that I still feel that way about him, even now, even after everything. I wanted him to know that love never dies. It just loses its voice." She shook her head. "That's corny."

"If he reads your book, he'll know."

"He won't read it, not now. Not if I'm on *Ellen*. Not if they make a damn movie out of it. Not if everyone on social media starts broadcasting every little detail about him and me, about the bad times. Everything is going to get all twisted, blown out of proportion. No one's going to know how sweet he can be, how goofy he is, how he made me laugh, that he listened, really listened, that he got me. We fought all the time, but we always made up. That will get lost. You know how people are. They're going to make him into a monster. It could kill his career. Everything he's sacrificed for." She was gripping his forearm now.

Samuel didn't know what to say.

"I shouldn't have put all that sex in there," she said, letting go of his arm.

"Sex—"

"Sells," finished Ashley. "I know, I know. People love a scandal. A serious writer like Price dating a former prostitute—a real *Pretty Woman* story." She looked up at the building. "That's why you sold it. Not because of me, because of him, because it exposes him." She looked down to the street, then out at the people passing by. "I just wanted to get his attention."

21

"You thought a memoir was the best way to do that?" asked Samuel. "What about a phone call?"

Ashley turned but looked through him. She was lost in thought. "Maybe he'll be proud of me." She shrugged her shoulders. "Proud of me for beating the odds. For making it. One more thing we have in common." She breathed in and looked at Samuel. "Thanks for listening. Go to your meeting."

"If *Ellen* calls, I'll let you know."

Ashley rolled her eyes. "Yeah, guess I'll start fasting." She turned and walked away from him, her long hair billowing in the wind like a black flag. She reached up and yanked it down.

The Coyote & Death

Will was exhausted.

He dropped the canvas "sea bag" on the metal shelf that would be his bed for the rest of his life, however long that might be. He gripped two threadbare sheets and a pillow in his other hand. These he dropped next to the sea bag, careful to keep his elbow pinned to his side, so as not to let his mattress slip.

"The appeal process," said his lawyer, Sandra Romain, leaning into him at the defendant's table, her hand on his forearm, "can take as little as three years." She looked at him, her tigress eyes searching.

His eyes, the eyes of a lamb being led to slaughter, could not keep hers. He could only stare at the judge's gavel, at the hand hovering impatiently above. The sound of the judge's voice echoed in his mind. He replayed, as a means of masochistic amusement, the downward strike, the judge's firm grip, the authoritative crack of wood-on-wood.

"Guilty."

"I could drag it out to ten," said the tigress.

"Please don't."

Will breathed in and out. He studied the fractured surface of the wall above his bed. The network of lines resembled those that appear, after a hundred years or so, in the varnish sealing the old masters' canvases. He let the inch-thick, vinyl-coated foam mat, his "mattress," slide from under his arm.

The six-by-ten space was caustic with an institutional smell; a mixture of body odor, stale air, dust, and disinfectant. The walls were white, antiqued by time. Bits of tape and putty marked where previous inmates had hung posters, pictures of family, or inmate artwork, sometimes erotic, but often not. He looked down. The words *Rzeczpospolita Polska* were printed on the side of the bag in faded black ink. The bag had been bought on remainder from the government of Poland.

Below that was a second stamp, the ink somewhat fresher. "B.O.P." Will knew what the acronym stood for: Bureau of Prisons. Like the "sea bag," like everything in the eight-by-ten cell, Will was the property of the B.O.P.

The trial was a formality. He'd known that. At first, he felt entitled to a trial, to a spectacle. Later, he felt detached. The drama had to play out. He had to defend his so-called innocence. Sandra fought valiantly. In her opinion the police had made grave misjudgments. Not only that, she was certain that the evidence had become tainted.

"That's how we're going to beat this, Will."

He hadn't taken it as a promise. Nor did he deny her the hope that she alone held for him. He'd never admitted to her, or to anyone else, that he was indeed guilty. He could have said it and avoided the trial. He couldn't. By the time he felt able to, events were already in motion.

His thinking about his actions had evolved. There's plenty of time for introspection while awaiting a trial whose outcome was life or death. He found it—not amusing, but perhaps ironic—that a man was finally able to think, to have the time to think, once all rights and responsibilities had been stripped from him.

He didn't concern himself overmuch with guilt or innocence. What was done was done. The rest of it was show. Since he wasn't taking the stand, it felt like the show wasn't even for him. Despite the forking paths before him, he was not to choose. He had been in a state of high stress for weeks. He wasn't yet resigned to his fate, despite being certain of it. If he was honest with himself, he was afraid.

Afraid of what? Death?

Seems a silly thing to be afraid of.

Afraid of being condemned?

Aren't we all?

His fellow inmates, men that spanned from the cowardly to the fearless, treated him with something approaching respect. He'd been spared the usual theft of commissary. He showered in peace. He was even "given" a portable CD player with headphones, a prized item. Of course, should he go free, or be sentenced and moved, the player would remain in B House.

A strange ritual had taken place when he returned from the courthouse and his sentence was known. The inmates gathered around him. It was a rare spectacle to see a living dead man. They followed him to his cell. They spoke for his belongings, negotiating, as if he had already passed from among them.

With an air of profound aloofness he handed out his few belongings and remaining commissary. He could take almost none of it from B to D, for death row was a universe unto itself. He would be given new clothes, not orange, the color of the sun, of fire, of life.

Prometheus, the thief of fire.

To be now like gods.

Eternal suffering at the will of Zeus.

No, not orange, the color of the uniforms worn by those who might one day breathe free air, but white, like a ghost, to whom a future is denied, to whom the past is an anchor. He kept only letters, pictures, and his books. Fellow artifacts from the past. Those inmates who had taken the time to learn his name and a few facts about his situation, shook his hand, touched his shoulder, made sure to meet his gaze.

The walk from general population, into the bright sunlight of the yard, then into the gloom of D building, was the most transcendent experience of his life. It was on that walk, waiting for mechanically sealed doors to open and close, that he had breached the barrier between the living and the dead.

I came to myself in a dark wood, for the straight way was lost.[1]

He pushed the *Rzeczpospolita Polska* to the side and sat down on the metal shelf. He turned and looked to the window. The glass was transparent, an inch thick, with a metal mesh embedded in it. Will looked to the terrain beyond. A dusty plain spread until it was washed out by the haze of the sun. He thought of Sir Thomas More's view from the Tower of London.

But now, my good Uncle, the world is here waxen such, and so great perils appear here to fall at hand, that methinketh the greatest comfort that a man can have is when he may see that he shall soon be gone.[2]

The remains of pale-yellow corn stalks extended from the dark earth. The sun turned them white, turned them into miniature tombstones. Soon, snow would come. Will wondered if he would see deer. He would certainly watch the corn grow with a sense of jubilation.

He blessed whomever had made the decision to allow transparent glass. B House had opaque glass. He had considered that a form of mild cruelty. He wondered if transparent glass, and a view, no matter how dismal, which allowed the imagination an opportunity to exercise itself, would have cut down on the relentless infighting he had witnessed in B House.

No. Immaturity is the dominant factor.

He had not yet spoken to anyone on death row. He would eventually, they too received yard time, although it was in a separate yard, away from the general population.

---

[1] Dante, *Inferno.*

[2] From a letter written to More while he was awaiting trial.

He was curious if the men of death row were more mature. He wondered if the trial and condemnation to death by his "peers" had a universal effect on man.

Look at you, Will. Doing it again. Always the aloof one, aren't you? Always looking at your own situation like an impartial scientist, or a martyred philosopher.

He closed his eyes and transported himself back to the courtroom, to the very moment the judge looked at him, before reading the sentence, before taking up his gavel. His eyes said it all, conferred judgment well before a word was spoken. Will had tried to predict how he might feel at that moment. He couldn't decide. As it turned out, he felt almost nothing. No rush of tears came, no sadness, no anger, no disappointment.

It wasn't until he was in the elevator, being taken down to the garage, where the prison transport was, that he felt the first emotion he was consciously aware of. That emotion was satisfaction. It surprised him to feel it. He expected anything else but that. He knew that he was guilty. He had done what he had done. He didn't regret it, not in a moral sense. He believed in justice. That's why he'd done it. That's why he couldn't leave it to others. To face his own justice felt appropriate, if displeasurable. Relief followed. He was relieved to have the trial over with. It wasn't until he saw the faces in B House that real emotion came. Those "hard men" wore their hearts on their sleeves. That got to him, pulled him down from his aloofness, confronted him with his reality.

"Fuck," he said aloud, to stop the memory from overwhelming him.

He rose from the metal shelf and walked to the metal sink, turned on the water, cupped his hands, filled them, and splashed the cool water on his face. He looked into the metal square glued to the cinder-block wall. A blurred, blue-hued face stared back at him. There was a knock at the door. The noise, although soft, rebounded around the room. He glanced at the door, through the window, but didn't see anyone.

"Yes?"

"Will." The sound was compressed, having squeezed through the gap between door and wall. "Come to the door."

Will wiped his hands on his pants and walked to the door. He looked through the window and saw the warden, who did not return his gaze. He was looking at a third man.

"Will, this is Dr. Durling."

Dr. Durling was shrunken with age; wisps of white hair adorned his head like laurel. Round-rimmed glasses hung from a lanyard around his neck, along with his ID card. He wore a dark blue V-neck sweater over a white shirt and a dark blue tie.

"Will," continued the warden, "Dr. Durling is a psychologist. Would you like to speak with him?" The warden glanced out of the corners of his eyes at Will, then looked back to the doctor.

Will thought before speaking. This second ritual surprised him almost as much as the one in B House. "I imagine the suicide rate for inmates on death row is higher on the first day."

"Are you feeling suicidal, William?" asked Dr. Durling.

Will waited a few moments before answering. "Render therefore unto Caesar the things which are Caesar's; and unto God the things that are God's."

The warden turned and walked away. Dr. Durling watched him go then turned and looked at Will. "What do you mean by that, Will?" he asked in the same gentle, guiding tone.

"No, Doctor, I am not suicidal," said Will. "Thank you." He turned and walked to the window, leaving the doctor to look at his back.

"One piece of advice, William." Dr. Durling's voice floated into the room, filled it, like sweet incense. "Make plans. Even here a man can accomplish much. 'For God hath not given us the spirit of fear; but of power, and of love, and of a strong mind.'" He paused, letting the words take effect.

Will turned his ear to the door.

"I am always available to speak, William. Should you desire it."

Will returned his gaze to the blank plain, to the sun-whitened stalks.

Dr. Durling departed.

Silence returned.

How would a man kill himself in here?

Will looked around to room.

What exactly is at his disposal?

He walked over to *Rzeczpospolita Polska* and fingered the ends of the drawstring.

Two feet, perhaps.

The spirit of fear.

He looked to the door again. Through the window he saw the edge of the steel door opposite him. It was painted institutional green; pale, milky, like the walls of an insane asylum.

Ten years?

…and of a strong mind.

He looked to the drawstring. He thought of Sir Thomas More, who wrote beautifully while imprisoned in the

Tower of London, before Cromwell denied him his papers, the greater crime.[3]

What do I have to say?

Will turned back to the empty field. A flicker of movement caught his eye. A coyote, full-bodied from a summer of plenty, his gray-white coat reddened by the sun, dark, expressive eyes, entered into Will's field of vision. Will stepped closer, leaned into the glass, supporting himself with his hands pressed against the wall.

Have I ever seen a coyote?

…and of love.

The coyote trotted along the edge of the field. It entered the ditch separating the field and the perimeter road. It stepped up onto the road, paused, and looked around. It was directly in front of Will now, perhaps twenty yards away. Only the electrified fence kept the coyote from advancing further. The coyote sat at the edge of the road. It bent forward and sniffed the ground. It lifted its head and sniffed the air. Will leaned back and moved his hand. He closed an eye and positioned his finger.

I'm Will.

The coyote sniffed him.

Shall I name you Sir Thomas More?

The coyote looked to his right, rose, and ran off in the other direction. Will let his arm fall to his side. A moment later the perimeter truck crept into view. A guard leaned forward, looking with interest at the coyote.

Don't let them get you, Sir Thomas.

---

[3] Sir Thomas More wrote *A Dialogue of Comfort Against Tribulation* while imprisoned in the Tower of London, 1534. Upon hearing that More had papers and books, Oliver Cromwell, who was acting as prosecutor, took them away.

The truck crept out of view. Will walked to the metal shelf. He bent and retrieved the mat. He picked up the *Rzeczpospolita Polska* and leaned it against his leg. He set the sheets and the pillow on top. He placed the mat in its place. He gathered his linens and set them aside. He pulled the drawstring, opened the bag, and began to unpack.

I'll get a legal pad and pencils tomorrow. Maybe I'll have something to say by then, Sir Thomas.

The Products

Anita woke from a nightmare and reached for her phone. Consciousness came to her, and she wondered why she was holding it. She recalled the contents of her dream. In the nightmare, she was no longer associated with a product. Her particular product was the Revere® Clean Pan™ 6.5-quart Hard Anodized Aluminum Non-Stick Stock Pot with Lid & Pasta Insert, suggested retail price, $87.99.

She began to access her various social media accounts to check her long-standing association with her self-identified product, a brand relationship that realized and communicated something deep, intangible, and personal. Everyone had a product, "their product." It had unsettled her to dream of the absence of her product. She had grabbed her phone to reassure herself that the relationship still existed. She realized she had to pee.

For a moment, she contemplated taking her phone with her to the toilet. She felt it would be a bit too obsessive and set her phone on the nightstand. She got out of bed and shuffled down the hall to the bathroom. She stared, blank-minded, at a patch of gray moonlight on the wall as she peed. She left the bathroom, stood in the hall, but not turning towards her bedroom. Instead, she turned towards the kitchen and found the light switch in the dark.

Her eyes burned with the harsh light. She squinted and blinked until she grew accustomed to it. She looked on top of the refrigerator. There it was, the Revere® Clean Pan™ 6.5-quart Hard Anodized Aluminum Non-Stick Stock Pot with Lid & Pasta Insert, suggested retail price, $87.99. She tilted her head and studied it. The black of the anodized body was not as crisp as she remembered. It was dusty. The shimmer of the aluminum pasta insert, she had always adored the contrast between the mysterious, void-like black body and the brilliant, star-like insert, was dull, the life gone from it.

"When's the last time I used you?" she asked her beloved product. She remembered a recent criticism that had come from her closest friend, Jeanette.

"It's colloquial."

"Huh?" Anita inquired.

"Plebeian."

Anita looked at her, still confused.

"Commonplace, everyday. It's blue-collar. What are you, an old, married biddy?" Jeanette had looked over her glasses as she spoke, like a scolding schoolteacher. "Besides, it's a little demeaning."

"What do you mean?"

"Well," Jeanette shrugged her shoulders, "you went to college, you have a good job, you're smart and independent. You're a small-f feminist."

"And—"

"Cookware? Really?"

She had punched Jeanette in the arm. "I like to cook! I can be a small-f feminist and still like to feed people! Bitch."

She laughed, but she was hurt. How many times had Jeanette helped her extend her brand? How many times had Jeanette re-posted some recipe that, for best results, required Anita's product? It felt like her best friend had second-guessed her choice of husband. Now she was second guessing.

She thought of Jeanette's product, the Rotring Rapidograph Pen - 0.2 mm - Black Ink, suggested retail price, $36.00. She began to understand the product in a new way, to understand Jeanette in a new way. 'It's assertive,' she thought. 'It makes permanent marks. It can't be erased. It's confident. It's masculine.' She frowned. 'No, not masculine, it's big-f feminist.' Anita suddenly became self-conscious. She turned out the light, no longer wishing to look at the pot collecting dust on top of the fridge.

Anita crawled back under the covers. She tossed and turned. She thought of Jeanette and the Rapidograph. She slammed her head into her pillow. 'You stopped drawing after college. You use AutoCAD software now,' she silently accused her best friend. 'You keep that pen as your product out of nostalgia. I keep my pot out of nostalgia. It reminds me of my mother, is that so bad?' But it was too late to win an argument, even a one-sided argument. Her cherished product, which she had filled with her essence, she often felt, was now just a pot. 'It *does* make me sound like an old biddy,' she concluded. 'Damn it! She could've told me years ago!'

She reached over and grabbed her phone but didn't enter her password. 'Changing your product is such an undertaking,' she thought. 'It takes weeks of research, months. It takes serious soul-searching.' She looked at her phone and asked herself, 'what product best describes me at this juncture in my life?'

She knew her relationship with Revere® was over. She had once loved the old silver smith and Revolutionary War hero. She was overwhelmed with the historical background of her former product, it had lent her an air of honesty, forthrightness, even sturdiness, reliability, timelessness. The Revere Copper Company had been founded in 1801 by Paul Revere himself. It was two hundred years old! 'How long has the damn Rapidograph been around, Jeanette?'

Despite her emotion, it was too late. She was filled with resignation. She knew she would have to de-product herself. 'The nightmare comes true!' Her friends and family would want to know what happened. They would want to know why. Her mom would be aghast. She had been with the Revere® Clean Pan™ 6.5-quart Hard

Anodized Aluminum Non-Stick Stock Pot with Lid & Pasta Insert, suggested retail price, $87.99 longer than she had been with any man.

Then, after a respectful amount of time, she would start floating out potential associations. Would it be the Tiffany & Co. Classic Cloth Notebook, suggested retail price, $200.00 for a set of three? 'No, too pretentious.' Would it be the Acqua Di Giò Absolu scent, the top selling women's perfume by Giogio Armani, suggested retail price, $72.00 for a 1.4 oz. bottle? 'God, no. I'd probably lose friends!'

She typed in her password and went to her social media accounts. There it was, her beloved product. She felt like she was looking at photographs of an ex-lover. Perhaps wishing to torture herself, she clicked over to Jeanette's profile. "What!" she said out loud. The Rotring Rapidograph Pen - 0.2 mm - Black Ink, suggested retail price, $36.00 was completely absent from her profile! Not even a ghost of it remained, not a word, not a whisper. She searched her various accounts. Gone.

There was nothing, nothing at all. It was as if Jeanette and the Rapidograph had never been. Then, like a miracle, a new product appeared. The Michael Kors Collection Simone Swarovski® Crystal Clutch. She read the description. Suggested retail price, $2,990.00. "What?" Anita yelled. "Oh—you bitch. You fucking—a clutch! A fucking three thousand dollar clutch!"

Anita fumed. "What's all this bullshit about my product being demeaning? What are you, a trophy wife?" She growled into the phone-glow-lit-but-otherwise-empty room. 'Oh! From Rapidograph to Swarovski® Crystal Clutch.' She shook her head as she watched the new product populate Jeanette's various online accounts. 'Adding two zeros to your product cost, are we? And in the middle of the night!' She knew Jeanette had intentionally broken-up with her product and replaced it in the middle of the night so that the first thing everyone saw when they woke up was her fantastic new relationship.

In an irrational fury of emotions and keystrokes Anita emptied her accounts of Revere® and everything associated with it. An evil smile spread over her face as she effortlessly replaced her former product. After the hard break was accomplished, after the new product was spread like rat poison in every nook and cranny of her online life, she turned off her phone and lay her head down on her pillow, satisfied.

'The Michael Kors Collection Simone Swarovski® Crystal Clutch, suggested retail price, $2990.00.' She smiled in the dark. 'Versus the No Holds Barred Benelli M3 Tactical Semi-Automatic Shotgun, suggested retail price, blow it out your ass, Jeanette.'

H. Rad Bethlen has been compared to Isak Dinesen (*Seven Gothic Tales*) and Fritz Leiber (*Swords and Deviltry*). He is known for his work in the fantasy and horror genres as well as his non-fiction. He has been published in Europe and America.

Enjoy these stories?

If you liked what you read, please take a moment to **leave a review on Amazon**! Your feedback helps other readers find these stories. It only takes a minute but it makes a huge difference. The Amazon algorithm requires 30-50 reviews before it will pick this book up and promote it to like-minded readers. Your review is instrumental in helping that happen!

For more great fiction and non-fiction please visit:

roosterandravenpublishing.com

hradbethlen.com

or H. Rad Bethlen's Amazon page.